AF434803

Prologue

Angry cries bounced off the walls and followed me through the palace.

Their armor clad bodies struggling to keep up with my agility, as I swerved in and out of the dark crevasses willing my body to comply with me. God this would be so much easier if I could just keep his defined muscles and godly complexion away from my mind, if I was in a less stressful situation I could let my imagination come up with all sorts of things or certain body parts to be specific.

But I don't need him or his kindness anymore. I'd done it. And they knew they knew I'd stolen it. There wasn't much need for stealth I took it right from underneath their snobby noses. Id stolen what was presumably the most precious and desirable object in the whole of rose wood I'd stolen the goblet its mine all mine.

Heart pounding, sweat pumping I turned the corner expecting to await my most trusted stead, but as I came to a haggard stop I realized I was never escaping for he was there. A sly smile playing on his face as he held his blade to my throat. Atlas.

Chapter one

Poets manipulate words to form an illusion of reality, sculpting it until its unrecognizable, setting standards and causing an addiction to their false realms and fantasies making us believe in the unbelievable and forcing us to accept that their versions of reality will always be just out of reach always non tangible always be fiction.

That's what I would tell you if I could read, or if I had parents to teach me.

Rolling my eyes, I hoped off the rock I was perched on and made my way to the closest stream, perks of being an orphan in a forbidden forest is I can get naked whenever I want and have no shame about it.

I drink the cold river water like it's going out of style. My gulps are so large the noise is more like a seal swallowing a fish. I look up to see a billion verdant wands of pine waving in the air; for this place is magical so much so that I can feel it from my core to my fingertips. From the rich purple hues of the forest ground to the sweetness of the blue-white sky, the forest is my three dimensional wonderland for the eyes who are willing to absorb the light.

I must admit sometimes I yearn to leave the premesis to socialize with others but that's what the market in florescent hollow Is for. Sure it's full of arrogant pricks but they have amazing fruit and vegetable stalls. Although I don't have a source of income my stealth and powers come in handy.

I doubt I'll ever get caught they can't even enter my court let alone track my powers back to any sort of hollow, I'm blessed with supernatural abilities from every court I'd like to see those bastards try.

Chapter two

Atlas.

My father slammed the whiskey on the table tiny droplets cascading and dampening the table we sat at.

"damned thief" he yelled

Earning a flinch from mother. He was drunk you could smell the alcohol on his breath, he always has excuses as to why his in this position todays one is the thief. To be more exact the thief of rose wood who has been plaguing our lands and scaring away street vendors with their cunning precision.

Some claim the thief is a woman others disagree proclaiming only a man would have such a skill set. A very few set of subjects believe it's the ghost of a poor child who died of starvation. Do with that information as you please. For it might help my father get his head out of the whiskey cabinet and back into running the kingdom.

"calm down albert your scaring the kids" mother said barley audibly.

Ah yes the 16 and 17 year olds still kids in the eyes of my deranged mother. I mean when is she going to wake up and realize she is slowly killing herself with this violent repulsive excuse for a man. Actually on the contrary if someone offered me power in this patriarchal land I would take them up on the offer even if I had to marry a woman like my father.

I brought my focus out from my thoughts and rejoined the conversation.

"son," my drunken father drawled through slurred tones "you will find this scum and you will kill them do I make myself clear? If you're going to rule this kingdom you're going to need the public to view you as a success, a grand ruler" "sure just like how they view you" I mumbled sarcastically under my breath. If my father heard it he made no reaction, probably too drunk to register it.

my father gave a hateful glance to my sister preparing to attack her with any sort of devious words he has in his arsenal. That's the way of our people in Atlantis manipulative and wise.

My hold on my power slipped ever so slightly causing a soft rumble to shake the castle I gave a stern look to my father,

"if you ever even think of laying your hand on your child then I will show you exactly how I execute punishments in my prison"

If terror could possibly ever take form and present its self my father's face would be the portrait he'd choose as inspiration. he left the dim living room without even so much as a grunt for he knew I would easily beat him and probably kill him if I felt like it.

Ever since I was little he knew he couldn't break me no matter how hard he tried, I've been broken for years but there will be a day when I will gladly break him.

"If the goodness of the monarchy does not out shine the gold and jewels of the palace, then let it stand empty until true royalty arrives "is what the pope once shouted to my father its words once again ring truth in my head as I cross the large perimeter of the palace to my room. I must admit the palace is grand and all but it's not the place for lords to talk of what matters to the community or how to create a healthier nation. it's a place used for parties, for rich people who don't know what to do with the large amount of money they possess. These people do not care that the damn public is so poor people are dying rapidly for no other reason than for my father's unique ability to turn a blind eye to what matters most.

Movement in my peripheral vision caught my attention. The guards were armoring up and getting ready to go into town.

"wait" I sprinted over and informed them of my sudden need to go to the market using a lame excuse to cover up the fact I'm only trying to get a lead on this thief. With weary glances at each other they relented and let me tag along. Perfect. Now I can execute my devious plan to finally kill this monster.

Chapter 3

Astrid.

Being hungry is a thing most mature adults can endure for at least several hours. It's only been five hours since I've been to the market and yet again I'm starving. So yet again, I have to travel to florescent hollow.

The path doesn't care about the terrain that's for me to deal with. The path is the path. So whatever comes I keep going. The wind is relentless but it separates to let me pass. The forest has a soft spot for me if it didn't I'd most likely be dead by now.

Crossing the border without getting caught Is the hard part the guards are so arrogant they think every girl they meet falls in love with them. No other court has egos as high as the almighties. My shabby blonde hair blows into my face as I creep closer to the border I can already smell the sweet honeysuckles and strawberries. The aroma is suffocating in a sweet sickly way. Making me want to gorge myself on all the produce.

Luckily the guards don't anticipate someone emerging from behind, since no one in their right mind would ever enter the forbidden forest. Slowly I slipped under the gates and into a nearby bush. The sun seemed to burn righter here as if even he felt egotistical shining down upon florescent hollow.

Walking up the hill to the market, I see families carrying woven bags of apples and greens. Smiling and laughing. I try to picture what my family would be like, mother rubbing my back after I've been sick or father sneaking me out late at night to go shopping. Would we have been as joyful as them? Would my parents provide for me and cherish me? Would they love me?

Before I became completely vulnerable to my crushing emotions I pulled my head out the clouds and into game mode. Today I felt like having some cucumber and cheese. So I made my way to sweet talk Maggie.

"hey ma- "I began before I realized she was staring quite openly at some thing or should I say someone. Confused I followed her gaze to the middle of the square where a group of guards stood. Shit. I can't steal crap all with them there.

Sighing I walked solemnly down a nearby alley getting ready to have a big sulk when a man's silhouette drifted into my vision. I opened my jaw to scream as he speedily approached. He clapped a calloused hand onto my mouth before anything audible came out.

"shh, calm down I'm not going to hurt you girl" his voice slowly caressed my ears soothing my nerves as he gingerly released his grip on my face.

"you hiding from the guards too" I started

He gave me a confused look before a mask of complete indifference replaced it.

"why yes I am, and why may I ask are you hiding from them?"

I struggled to come up with an answer that could fool him, and ended up saying the first thing that came to mind

"my mother is afraid they'll take me away or something stupid she's always worrying."

"understandable they are quite fearsome, where bouts you from you don't look like you're from around these parts."

I had to think about my reply carefully especially since I could barely see this man, I could just about make out his bright purple eyes and what seemed to be dark hair. An atlantian. These people where not to ever be trusted. I've heard many a tales from gossip in the market about how cunning they are. So I lied. Maybe that also made me non-trustable.

"no, I'm from crystal hollow I've just travelled here to find a good teacher for my healing skills" it was believable enough I did possess the pale skin and light hair of the crystallite folk though the features of his face pulled into a questioning expression. He didn't believe me.

"sure darling," he said with a sly smirk "and I'm from florescent hollow"

I looked him up and down this guy was definitely not from here.

Bang! "there he is" shouted a gravelly voice from the entry way of the alley

I was about to leave him to sort this shit for himself when he picked me up and took off with me on his shoulder. Atlantian brute.

Chapter 4

Atlas

I've unfortunately bumped into one of the most peculiar girls, on my hunt for the thief. Her hair was long and untamed. Her eyes a deep blue. She looked home less the last thing I expected to do was pick her up and throw her on my shoulders in a wave of panic at being discovered.

God she was so light and frail it was vile. Do her parents not feed her? Maybe her parents are like mine? She has all the signs. Wariness, reluctance to trust, lying and my all-time favorite wit. The girl had wit. I could probably be able to stand the thing if she had a bath and ate something.

She must have been in shock at this sudden show of protection because she went rigid and seemed to be refusing to breathe in air. god this girl is annoying.

But she knows her way around these streets. I could tell by the way she knew I didn't belong straight away. She could help me find this thief and kill them at last.

Although she looked like she'd bathed in soot for the past six years she had this earthy, flowery scent, it wafted in my nose as she bounced from where she was positioned on my shoulder. It kind of turned me on in a weird way. God this girl is going to be the death of me.

But making friends of foes is the art of a moron. We have nothing in common we cannot be friends. The only thing we have that's similar is our ability to deceive people.

Wait. That's it we are both masters of deception and lies if we teamed up we could find this thief in no time. But if I reveal my true identity she will never trust me. Its fine ill come clean once the thief is dead.

It's like my mother used to say: don't trust people to much salt looks a lot like sugar.

"if you don't put me down I'm going to vomit all over your flashy top" the heathen croaked.

I grabbed her straw like arms and flung her on the dirt path, behind a fruit stall. Pushing her filthy head down to avoid catching the guard's attention. At least she was smart enough to comply. We were still out in the open we needed to be better hidden in case the stall vender caught us so we rubbed the pungent mud on our faces and hands. Then climbed into a natural hollow in the ground.

I watched her in faint amusement as she piled leaves and sticks on top of herself, not bothering to cover me. When she was finished she was perfectly hidden. She would likely have a high risk of getting trod on though. Idiot.

Chapter 5

Astrid.

"I hate you" I don't usually use such a strong word but it suits this situation perfectly "hate, my friend, is the devils path, and we shall leave its ash-strewn surface without a single foot print. hate brings only pain and the cycles of destruction upon us all" he whispered sorrowfully while watching his fingers play upon his lap. Collecting dirt, the more he did so.

Well that shocked the shit outa me when did this man become a poet, and why did he get so offended when I said I hated him. it's not like my opinion matters to him he just basically kidnapped me or maybe he saved my life. I haven't quite come to terms about what's happened yet.

He turned his face to me and I finally got a good chance to take in his features, and wow. There are many kinds of beauty as there are leaves in the autumnal forest, but his was more like the sharp cut edges of glaciers or the predatory gaze of a mountain lion. his beauty was god like and irresistible.

If he had better taste, better manners, better respect for women I couldn't think of a reason I should not like him. I wonder if my mother would approve? I have so little memories of her.

I flushed pink when I realized I was staring, I found him attractive and he knew it too. Arrogant prick.

"guards won't stop searching till sunrise so get comfy darling" he wound his muscled arms behind his head as a temporary pillow.

"I'm not sleeping in this close proximity to you" I proved my point by shimming to the opposite side of the hole.

"why? Because you can't control yourself and might start uncontrollably kissing me?"

"no I'm getting murderous thoughts you egotistical disgrace of a man"

We laid there on opposite sides neither one of us saying a word. Until sunset blossomed upon the clouds as sweet wild peonies doused in red and gold.

I felt him shuffle and heard leaves crunching and twigs snapping. I do strive to maintain patience but it's terribly hard when the animal next to you is astronomically loud.

"shut up for crying out loud" I screeched as I whipped my head around. Crap. Holy crap.

The atlantian hot guy [who I haven't got the name of yet] was pressed entirely up against the side of the hole. Giving me the most hateful glare in all of history. Opposite him was a huge, fearsome wolf.

It moved with predatory slowness showing its white-silver fur glossy and thick in the last slither of light in the sky. Its paws kiss the earth with a lightness ready to pounce. I stay still, I breathe slow any sudden moves and I would be a rotting carcass by morning.

There's a kind of fast movement that is precise and well thought through like the calculation of a chess player. Well this man's moves where not that, it was impulsive and god damn crazy. He stood on the side of the hole on higher ground and started waving his arms around like the drunken dance of an alcoholic. His going to kill the both of us. Maybe I could escape while its distracted?

Just as I was about to make a run for It the wolf whined and ran away.

"were you really going to leave me? I haven't even gotten your name" a devious glint shinned brightly.

"yes I was, and the names Astrid"

"ah well mighty coward Astrid mines" he seemed to hesitate thinking thoroughly whether to trust me or not.

"atlas"

"hah, imagine being named after a book of the world"

"I'm just going to remind you I just saved your life darling"

"get over yourself"

"I suggest leaving this place it seems to be a hotspot for predators"

Atlas strode down the dirt path and down to a nearby stream not bothering to check if I followed. Which I did. Soles moving upon such solid ground, we made bold progress and was quite close to the stream already. Well rather atlas was since he decided he wanted to show off just how reliable his muscles are and leave me meters behind. Prick.

He peeled off his jacket and placed it onto the trunk of a big oak tree. The tree leant into the moonlit rays as if they were lovers in an eternal trance. The ground beneath it seemed soft and grassy and maybe it was just the sleep deprivison but it looked softer than a cloud and the best place to lay my head and drift off to sleep.

I curl up next to atlas craving the warmth he is radiating. We are both barely conscious but before I drift off completely I feel the weight of his muscled arm curl around my waist. I'm too tired to care.

Chapter 6

Atlas.

He was dead. Father had killed him. I've never seen a dead person before and I never wished to again. I could only think about the life slowly leaving him as the blade punctured his flesh. The warm blood that caressed my feet. The slurred sound he mumbled as he slumped on the floor. The disdain on my father face as he beheld the mess on the marble.

He lashes out. Blames me. Because it's my fault. My fault that the servant had enraged father. My fault that tears pooled and burned my eyes showing my father the fear that controlled me in that moment.

He strikes me. At least he intended to. A buzz of power rumbled through me. I spied the soiled sword. One moment it was situated next to the corpse, the next it flew into the wall. Right beside fathers head. Omnikinesis. I had inherited the royal power. I was finally a match for my father. A wolf and a sheep.

I wake up suddenly, not because of any noise or disruption, yet because my dream had come to a conclusion. The play had ended and actors bowed now it was time to engage in the world once more. Starting with the mole rat curled up against me.

Pushing down the weight of the crushing memory, I took in the sight in front of me. The landscape had drastically changed. Last night it was grassy and full of fresh flowers that bathed in the moonlight. Now it was a dull barren land, the damned nightmares must have triggered my magic.

Now I have to deceit this girl into believing that this wasn't caused by godly power. That only someone as handsome and almighty as me could wield and manipulate, then she will never believe I'm not the prince. Fuck this was hard.

I peered down at her. I took in her freckles that were barely visible due to how dirty she was. Does her family not teach her about dignity?

He eye lids fluttered slightly and snowflakes seemed to dance around her finger tips, further proving my suspicions of her being from crystal hollow. The pointed tips of her ears seemed razor sharp in the beams of the sun.

I had to start executing my plan to team up before we separate or I'll never get the chance to find someone as trusting and street wise as her. She's the best chance I have.

"Astrid" I called, nudging her slightly as to not get any dirt on me.

The beast didn't even react.

"Astrid!" I raised my voice and sounded a lot like a mother scolding her child for misbehaving.

She drowsily turned her head to face me. "what?" she questioned frowning at the brightness of the morning.

"get your dirty self up, I've got something important to inform you"

"dirty? upon my skin is earth, that which sustains us. So call my appearance dirty if you require such cheap ego boosts, all this washes off, and beneath it I'm cleaner than you." She shot back before striking me with a surprising force.

I reeled back in surprise and actually laughed a bit at the nerve she had to attack a prince. Well she wouldn't be behaving like that if she knew I was royalty.

"I don't like hitting women but if you dare do something like that again then I will kill you" I growled.

She rolled her eyes and sat up, finally acknowledging the damage I'd done to the nearby land. Shock entered her expression and she whipped a confused head in my direction as if she knew I was to blame.

"what ha- "she started

"Never mind that I've got an important offer that I will not repeat, how would you like to team up with me to find and kill this thief?"

"no."

"I know we got off on the wrong foot but it's a well-planned elaborate scheme, I'm going to tell the town that I have a goblet in my possession that tells the past present and future. Its covered in jewels and probably worth more than the village. They will not be able to resist and will have to take it."

Her face was the picture of boredom until I mentioned the past present and future thing. Maybe there's more to this girl than meets the eye. What does she want to know?

"and why may I ask do you want me to help you? You certainly haven't been the nicest"

"well your my last option darling, I'm getting kind of desperate" laying my truths bare.

She smiled and it was the prettiest thing I've seen in a while, for it extended to her eyes. Blessed with purity unlike some. Maybe she wasn't so bad.

"ok ill help you on this ridiculous quest, but I doubt you could find her she's good at hiding."

"she?"

"well... you didn't expect a man to be so stealthy did you?" she replied a little too fast for my liking.

"well I don't suppose a woman could be smart enough to get away with it."

"patriarchal prick"

"we will meet up here tomorrow to find evidence and start the plan"

"fine what time?"

"sunset"

"ok"

"bye darling"

"see ya prick"

I watched her as she walked off into the woods. My heart ached at her absence. What's wrong with me?

I twist over and lean against the old oak. Yearning for her to come back for some weird reason. The light paints my skin warmly. I wonder how many hues of green my eyes are witnessing as I glance up at the abundance of foliage. Till tomorrow Astrid.

Chapter 7

Astrid.

I'm officially freaking out. People want me dead? I mean sure, I steal a few jewels on occasion and shiny things excite me but that's not an excuse to kill someone. And to top it off he thinks I'm gullible enough to fall for some shiny goblet. I guess I can point him in the wrong direction and further away from my forest. But that goblet. I need it. I need to know my past. I need to know what happened to my family.

Maybe if we get close he will let me indulge slightly on it.

If one is not curious, the learning has nothing firm to anchor to.

So maybe curiosity killed the cat, but it sure as hell won't kill me.

I Passed back through the village in the early beams of the morning sun. the village homes were stamped in the wide valley as if placed by some careful and meticulous collector.

The wind chattered through the streets, the rain danced upon rooftops and the sunlight contrived with the clouds to keep the village in ever glow. I ignored the gorgeous sights and focused on getting home otherwise I'd end up here forever.

Surprisingly, I made it to the border without any distractions, the guards were busy doing their usual poker games and getting drunk and if I'm lucky they'll start brawling over who's biceps are larger. It's comical really, their so large yet so dumb.

I cocked my leg up and hopped over the fence and into the forest. My home

Trudging through the mud of home, I let the droplets of rain caress my cheeks and drip on to the foliage below me. My mind kept uncontrollably leading back to atlas. There's something in the way he laughs that reminds me of my better self. The kind of creative brain that brings so much magic and interest to life, one that enjoys the sparking of ideas and schemes.

I sense he isn't a book with clean pages, similar to mine his had some hardships. I think that's why I feel so connected.

Climbing up into my elder oak tree I scrape my calloused hands on the aged bark while straining to reach my cluster of pillows and blankets that were layered on top of thick branches. My bed.

When the stars come out to play and evening turns to night, when the crickets sing, my bed awaits. I love the softness the quiet, the sense of rest. My safe space. My cozy serenity under the moonlight.

Placing my hands under my head I laid back and contemplated my elaborate plan. His already under the impression that the thief is a man so maybe I could manipulate his patriarchal thoughts even more to force him to believe it's a cunning, wise old man and send him on a wild goose chase.

Tomorrow I will convince the prick that I'm the furthest thing from a thief. But I'm defiantly getting my hands on that goblet.

Badass. I looked badass. Well if my reflection in the stream was anything to go by. My onyx corset was strung so tight I struggled to breath and my black leather leggings made my ass look more pronounced. Inky midnight boots hugged my feet and my pale hair was curled to perfection, as sunlit waves, as white lace the perfect kind of wild.

I couldn't help wondering if atlas would like it.

Stamping down the thoughts of him I strode out of the forest and made my way to the market.

The grass on my soles is soft on soft, a gentle tickle as each strand moves in the summer breeze as easily as my hair. I made my way to our spot where I found him strewn upon the trunk of the oak.

His eyes slowly drinking the sight of me. As if I was the sweetest flower and he was a starved bee.

Chapter 8

Atlas.

The attraction between us became a tangible thread in the air before we spoke a word.

Her long winter hair moved much as soft as beach grass in the wind swaying back and forth revealing and hiding her beautiful blue eyes which radiated every blue dancing sky and tranquil oceans from each pupil as if it were the most serine lake.

She adorned a black corset, it was a strong black, deeply soulful in the way all absolute things are. It was the sort of black that brought the silent music of the universe so deeply within one's core.

Her leather leggings clung to her curves and reflected the sun.

She looked hot. Very hot. Wait what am I saying. She's a commoner I must not associate or be attracted to her by any means. Why does she make me feel this way?

She looked different from the way she appeared the first time I met her. She no longer had the appearance of a wet mole rat and looked more like a…. queen.

"what?" she questioned with a raised eyebrow, when she finally arrived at our spot.

I moistened my lips and looked her up and down before shaking my head.

"we will begin our search in the florescent hollow village, its where they attack the most frequently."

She nodded in approval. Perhaps she'd been a victim of the thief's kleptomania.

"I've heard rumors that she lives in crystal hollow" she stated.

"why would she steal here when she lives overseas?"

"obviously she doesn't want people to suspect she lives there so she steals here to confuse and deceive us" she half-shouts.

"calm down darling, it's just a rumor and we can't travel overseas it costs too much, we are practically in the village so we will start there."

"ok" her lips thinned

Peculiar.

The village houses hugged together, sharing walls and forming a row of story brook perfect rooftop peaks, upon strong foundations, with bricks mortared together with loving hands.

We walked in unison, marking dark crevasses and alleyways.

I was mostly checking out the view and by "the view" I mean the sight of Astrid in those leggings. Damn. How's a man supposed to focus.

I tapped her shoulder and guided her to a nearby stall. We were not here to dally so I thought we should gather information from the vendors.

I could almost hear her heartbeat it was fast paced and felt like a caged beast savagely attempting escape. Was she... scared?

What does she have to fear?

"hello ma'am would you mind if I ask you a few questions on the thief?"

The woman looked displeased and turned her nose up at me. ME. The PRINCE. I could have her executed, but that would blow my cover instead I bowed my head in graciousness and strode off.

A screech pierced my ears.

She... she'd hit her. Her eyes expressed an emotion far more deadly than fury she was livid.

The woman's face was pale in contrast to the scarlet liquid dripping from her nose and onto the dirt where she lay.

I stood there in shock. Why did she hit her?

I decided I didn't care why, when I noticed a group of men gradually making their way towards Astrid.

I didn't think. I darted to where she was rooted to the spot and threw her onto my shoulder.

Flashbacks from when we first met made me quietly laugh like maniac while fleeing the village. Instead of kicking and screaming like the first time, she leaned into my touch and accepted it.

Chapter 9

Astrid.

I hit someone.

Fuck.

I don't know why I was even that angry, anger is a thing I channel into my emotions. I make it my rocket fuel to create a better world. Those times I have lashed out, lost self-control, I apologize and learn from that experience. Yet I felt no remorse punching that vile woman in her snobby fat nose.

Finally peering up from where I hung my head in shame, I started registering the faces that glared at me with immense disgust and disapproval. I mean, I had just punched a beloved villager in the face, but she deserved it.

People spat at atlas's feet (because mine were in the air) and he let out a harsh growl that made them move back a few paces as an onyx mist coated the tips of his fingers. My embarrassment faded into fear. As if he could sense my change in emotions the mist dissipated completely.

Heavy footsteps thudded behind us. Oh shit. In all my panic I never noticed the two guards that were chasing us. Fuck. How are we going to get out of here if I don't use my powers. Ok just this once ill change the terrain so we can escape.

I reached out into my inner source. Passion and obsession, single minded and focused. See me in the light or the shadows, because what I see is a reflection of me. So magic are you empathetic for a poor girl or are you cold and want to leave me to be hanged? Hoping for the former I flung myself off of atlas' shoulder. He gave me an incredulous look that swiftly morphed into shock as the dirt began rising, filthy auburn rocks glued together and dust particles collided and began gradually creating a wall of solid rock.

The footsteps halted in their chase as they could not overcome the obstacle before them.

Atlas' brows creased and he looked utterly baffled. I watched him warily as he stared blankly at his hands turning them over and studying them. What was he going to think of me now? What if his figured out I'm the thief? Oh no. no. no. no.

I'm starting to hyperventilate, oh god.

Chapter 10

Atlas.

I'm frozen solid. A statue. Solid like the wall before me.

Where the fuck did that come from?

The sickly sweet aroma of magic filled my lungs. Strong magic

Omnikinisis.
My power.

I must have loosened my grip on my magic in my frantic attempt at escape. The heart pounding ferociously on the barrier of my skin reminded me of the severity of the situation.

Shit. I need an excuse to explain the wall.

I opened my mouth to explain the exact moment she did.

"that was…"

"erm so…"

Looking up I noticed our expressions were identical. In this moment time seemed to slow as we just stared at each other. I gobbled up the sight of her. The intricate constellation of freckles that adorned her forehead. The ocean blue swirls of her eyes and the petite nose in the middle of her face, that contrasted with her full lips that made me want to kiss so badly. if Looking at her like this was a sport it would be my hobby. I unexpectedly wanted to hide her away proclaim she was mine and kill anyone who dared come close. In this moment I could watch her for a lifetime and trace circles on her back connecting the moles that flourished on it.

Drunken on her complexion I snap myself out of my dazed state and rejoined reality. Astrid seemed unaware of my ogling but her cheeks where flushed a tint of pink. Was she dreaming of my complexion as well?

It doesn't matter I told myself.

"are you just going to stand there and check me out all day or are you going to get your ass in gear and get out of here before the guards find a way to get over that wall"

Kicking my shin and giving me an agitated look she gestured to the path beside us and we took off running.

Bending beneath washing lines and dodging a horde of children leaving a nearby church we made our way to the edge of the village.

Panting and struggling for air, we made it. She was a floppy sack on the floor and she refused to get up. Shows how much exercise she does, I thought rolling my eyes. I however stole this moment to flex my biceps and pretend that lengthy sprint affected me only slightly.

"come on it wasn't that hard darling"

"shut. The fuck. Up."

Turning to face the woods to hide my smile I took in the view. And I couldn't help but think she made it appear better just by existing.

I Observed from the corner of my eye as she got up and joined my side.

"you know some days I wish I could just forget about being poor or having problems and just frolic in the woods enjoying the views and rejoicing in the abundance of foliage" she whispered solemnly.

This time I looked at her, really looked at her. She did the same. My gaze dropped to her lips as if in some sort of trance.

I lean in and gently guide her head toward mine. her eyes drift shut as she accepted my touch yet again. Our kiss lasts merely seconds but it feels great. Thousands of rational thoughts are pushed away and once her warmth is gone I crave more, but I restrain myself and remain a gentleman.

She blinks. And then blinks again. Her lips part as if to say something but she doesn't utter a word. She just gapes like a fish.

I scramble to find words or even an explanation for what just occurred but my mind is bare. The only thoughts that remain are how much I long to repeat our brief kiss and extend its lasting.

I moisten my lips, the lips that still taste like her.

"it's getting late I must be leaving"

"yes, yes ill just be erm… going too, goodbye"

"farewell" she says while staring pointedly at the ground. Fidgeting with a loose piece of string on her corset.

What I'd just done finally registered in my head. Fuck. I've just made out with my business partner. What's wrong with me?

It was impulsive and reckless but it felt right. Like a puzzle piece finally finding its place. Finally connecting, finally whole. Now I'm empty and alone without her here I'm a yin without a yang. A moon without my bright sun. my sun. mine.

She is like an addictive drug consuming every fiber of my being.

My charismatic, feisty, aggravating, compassionate Astrid. My love. I admit it. Finally, being genuinely truthful with myself. I'm in love with Astrid.

Does she feel the same?

Or is this all one sided?

Chapter 11

Astrid.

Love feels like the rise and fall of the ocean, the swells, the sounds of the waves crashing, knowing there is a huge risk within but also knowing there's treasure.

I like atlas. I mean like more than usual. More than friends. But he's always so cold to me I very much doubt he feels the same. And there's also the fact I'm the very thing he wishes to kill.

That may hinder any chance I have with him unfortunately.

He will never find out. I refuse to let that happen.

We are meeting tomorrow to search the northern part of fluorescent hollow so I must prepare to be manipulative, cunning and deceitful. Skills I have conveniently honed into perfection.

Sighing, I made my way to the barrier. The guards weren't at their usual posts. Probably at a tavern somewhere getting wasted. Shrugging I made my way to the gate getting ready to jump over when a crack of a branch being destroyed beneath something heavy rang in my ears.

Slowly. Ever so slowly I turned around ready to face whatever monstrous creature lurked behind me. Nothing. Not an animal nor fae were positioned behind me. Nerves. Must be nerves, after all, today was quite stressful.

I continued my attempt at climbing over the gate. But stopped a few seconds later because something was off. I glanced around, the lanterns where blown out on all the guards posts and the birds refused to enter the proximity. Strange.

WHOOSH!

 A straw bag was thrown and wrapped tightly onto my head. My breathing escalated and my pulse pumped feverishly. I couldn't see. Couldn't see the strong hands that grabbed my waist. I could only hear the snickers and muffled laughs of men. All of my senses were useless. I can't use my magic if I'm blind. So I used the only thing accessible. My voice. I screamed I buckled I kicked and shouted. Until my throat felt like sand paper and my legs where restrained.

"ATLAS!" I screeched. But it didn't matter they won. Nothing matters.

Chapter 12

Atlas.

Refusing to leave the spot of our kiss, I lounged on the soft grass watching butterflies collect pollen from nearby tulips.

Closing my eyes, I felt at peace. That peace only lasted two seconds unfortunately.

Loud shrieks of pure terror rattled my brain making me impulsively jump up and search for the owner of them.

"ATLAS!" they shrieked. Astrid.

Someone had hurt her. someone's going to die today and it's not going to be her.

I run, feet kissing the land. Perhaps a little while ago I would have balked at the idea of running so far and so fast, now I relish the prospect as my steps become faster for every scream she makes.

Propelling myself forward I try to calm myself. I tell myself she's fine she's ok, although I don't fully believe it. My only sense of guidance is her voice. A voice that has slowly depleted in its sound and has become scratchy and unrecognizable.

I arrive just as the screaming had resolved. Why is she at the border?

It doesn't matter, I tell myself as I spy the guards dragging her body to their wagon. My fury builds up, boils, bubbles above the surface. How dare they.

I focus on my core generating my anger into a useful weapon. Guiding it towards its target. The men may possess super strength but they are no match. Not a worthy enough opponent for what I've got in store for them. But for now they can sleep. Astrid is my top priority.

I approach swiftly and smoothly. Hitting a pressure point on the back of their necks which triggered them into a deep sleep I spat on their pathetic bodies and caught Astrid just as she was about to fall.

Sheepishly I pulled the bag off, expecting to see bruises and cuts but her skin was pristine. Angelic even. Must be her crystal hollow magic.

Lifting her limp body onto my shoulders, I comically realized that's all I seem to do. She makes me act weird. I walked at an average pace back to our spot. Ill question her later.

I laid her down on a soft bed of grass. Yawning, from the missed sleep.

I collapsed on the ground next to her and pulled her close to make sure no one would take her.

Chapter 13

Astrid.

The last thing I remember were warm muscular hands catching me.

I spring up, well at least I try to. Strong toned arms held me tighter in their grip. Refusing to release me. The wisps of the now moonlight paint light across his face.

"stay" he mummers "stay"

I lay my head down and sleep claims me.

Fatigued I opened my eyes and squinted at the bright beams of the sun.

Atlas' arm no longer possessed my waist and had moved to under his head, I felt a strange feeling of emptiness without it. A bee without its stripes.

Birds whistled merrily in the trees and it's almost a definite contrast of what last night was. Last night. I'd mentally blocked out that traumatizing experience, forced it out of my mind and down to the dark abyss of where lost memories lay and thrive.

My power source sends a soft hum down my spine, begging to be put to use, ready to ultimately cause my demise one day. Once my feeble eyes are adjusted to the lambent sun waves, I turned to see atlas studying me with sharp precision, not an ounce of humor graced his features but a sympathetic gleam shone in the softness of his magenta eyes. He was going to juice me dry of every detail of last night and need a good reason as to why the guards wanted to catch me and why I was at the border in the first place.

"it's early, go back to bed." He said softly

It cured my nerves so I let my heavy eyelids close and drift into unconsciousness, holding his hand for comfort.

When I awoke he was gone.

Chapter 14

Atlas.

I admit I do feel bad for leaving, but I've avoided my royal duties (just saying it makes me sick) for too long.

My father's probably taken the liberty on "educating" my sister on all the cruel ways we secured the crowns safety. Manipulating words and using them as weapons to control the loyal minds of the court, for even the ones closest to you have a better chance at stabbing you. Metaphorically of course. In some cases.

The palace has been my home for decade upon decade, and a small world unto itself. Yet when everyone turns their head to watch you pass, when your name is on a million lips, it is your world and that is all the place you have to exist as the real vulnerable version of yourself.

The diamonds sparkled like a thousand tiny droplets splattered against the wall, I run my hand along them, fingers tracing the unique intricate shapes.

Footsteps echoed down the hall. High heels, click clacking like maracas. Probably denting the marble but who cares when you can replace it with the click of your fingers?

Every miniscule sound had me discretely looking over my shoulder every minute.

For some unknown reason I felt on edge ever since Astrid got attacked. Tense, in case I heard her call and had to fight a million armies I was prepared. Prepared to do anything. Prepared for everything.

But what I was not prepared for was bumping into my father.

The crispness of his uniform was spoilt by the pungent smell of whiskey that didn't coincide with the formality of his clothes and attitude.

He looked me up and down and snickered, sly lips pulling up in a cruel mirthless smile.

"you haven't caught them yet have you?" he stated.

"maybe I have."

"son, your coronation is in four days. If you don't have them by then your head will never touch that crown. I will make sure of it."

I went to leave but he grabbed me. Plump fingers wrapped tightly around my arm. I felt my magic rumble. He let go.

"to prove you will actually end up catching them instead of lounging about, let's make an oath."

"an oath?" I said perplexed.

"yes."

"what are the circumstances?"

"you have to swear you will capture the thief and kill her on the sunset of your coronation"

"and if I do not?"

"you'll never be king"

I thought about my response carefully oaths are no small thing.

"fine" I resigned. It wasn't the worst thing I'd have to do. Trust me.

His meaty hands fished a miniscule dagger from his trouser pocket. Grunting when his finger got caught on a loose thread.

"I'll do the honors of going first my boy." I've never been a boy to my father, only a monster.

Father hesitated slightly before curving out a chunk of flesh.

"hurry and produce blood before mine hardens child."

I sighed incoherently and didn't hesitate before driving a deep wound, I ignored my fathers shocked expression and joined our fingers. Blood oath.

"I hear by grant a blood oath, to kill the thief of rosewood"

"if he does not complete the task something the same value will be collected in their place"

"what!!" furious I snatched my hand back in disgust. How dare he!

"you never mentioned that part" I said biting back my power as the palace grounds began to shudder. Ragged breaths were the only sound besides the trembling palace.

Then a sweet aroma entered my respiratory system stroking and soothing my anger until it sizzled out. Her scent. Roses. Tulips. Earth. Forest. Astrid. My Astrid.

I turned on my heel and left. Some would call me a coward but the wise would know that I'm just planning my version of karma.

My father knew. That's why he silently crept away. I could still hear his heart savagely pounding.

I must kill the thief at all costs.

The oak door of my room slammed shut.

I sigh and slouch in my chair while running my calloused fingers through my onyx hair.

The wind blew pages of research across the room. They floated like petals before losing momentum and falling. I watch them. The raven ink could be seen from the other side of the parchment. It read "evidence for the rosewood thief"

This is hard. Their too good. And my partners shit.

And I hate her. Hate her like the poor hate the rich. envy her like the elders the young.

But still I yearn for her. I've forgotten names of women of the past, but hers rings in my head like an elongated bell. Never letting me forget it. And maybe I don't want to forget this bell. Maybe I want to carry on chiming it. Who knows the constant chime may become comforting.

Not bothering to pick up the sheet I hurl myself onto my four poster, gold turret bed nearly slicing myself on the encrusted diamonds.

I remove my thin cotton shirt and flex the muscles on my back. Turning over I clamp my eyes down, trying to sleep. But sleep doesn't come. Black. Onyx. Abyss. That's what I see. All I see. No dreams or make-believe scenarios no traumatic memories resurfacing from the past.

Aggravated I kicked the sheets off of me. Golden threads twinkled in the candle light before adorning the hardwood floors.

What was that thing Astrid did to me to make herself fall asleep?

It was something comforting, something gentle. A soft graze.

Ah yes that was it, a delicate caress upon my index finger. Carefully I closed my lids and repeated the motion twirling circles upon my skin. Goosebumps followed soon after sprouting up like clovers in a bare field.

Finally, I was at peace and sleep hunted me down like a starved hound.

Chapter 15

Astrid.

Surprisingly I wasn't mad.

After being rudefully left at the tree like the vegetables on a kid's plate, I trudged miserably down the dirt path to my forest.

 The barrier loomed in the distance tall and foreboding. This time no guards awaited to drag me back, no dangerous creatures lurked, it was honestly a bore. I suppose everything seemed boring without him.

The fence seemed to pity me and open itself. Well at least that's wat I pretended happened.

I breathed in the sweet moist odor of my forest. candied honeysuckles and tulips. Frogs croaked a choir of different tones. Similar to the orchestra of crickets in florescent hollow but not the same.

I was just about to remove my rose colored top when a huge lump of coal attacked me. Vast onyx feathers fluttered softly as if exhausted after the apparently long journey away from its nest. A crow. A majestic species of bird.

I've never come across one before but I'm guessing their not usually this friendly. It's been spelled. Strong magic pulsated from the crow. Peculiar utterly peculiar.

"hello there darling" came atlas' voice from the beak of the crow.

"atlas are you in the bird?"

"if your receiving this message then my crow has done its job once again remarkable isn't he?"

It seemed this message was recorded in advance.

"I'm guessing you said yes. Meet me at our spot by noon."

No further message released its self from the crow. But still it stood there menacingly as if blaming me for him having to come all this way.

After looking me up and down in disdain he flew away. Midnight wings flapping with intensity.

My heart returned to its normal pace from the shock of the random bird after realizing atlas used magic. Powerful magic. Who is he?

For the first time in a while I was the first to arrive.

It was weird. It felt like something big was going to happen today, oh yeah, I'm going to get my hands on that goblet. I need to milk him on descriptions. He seems close to residents of the palace, judging by the amount of detail he presents me with.

A small figure began making its way towards me gradually taking shape of atlas.

He looked rough, well as rough as you can be when your perfect. His tousled black hair was dull and his clothing consisted of a black polo and midnight jeans.

"hello darling" drawled seductively but I was no fool. I could see right through his thorough disguise, he was upset.

"hey, you left me this morning, prick."

"duty called" he replied almost empathetically as he sat.

A crimson scab on the tip of his index finger caught my eye.

"what's that" I said concernedly grabbing it and inspecting the cut like a worried mother.

"thorn bush" he said with a nod towards nearby foliage. I wasn't fully convinced.

Just as I was about to join him on the grass the sound of squeaky wheels caught my attention.

I swiveled my head to glimpse a wagon. The majestic multicolored horses pulling it slowed to a stop when their owner pulled their reigns.

They halted a few yards back and we gawked as two Fae stumbled out of the scarlet and amber wagon. An elderly man and a woman.

The woman had a wide frame and brunette hair that swept against her ankles. It was braided in a plait that showed off her gray streaks, her head adorned a paisley scarf with tiny gold coins that framed her forehead.

The man, in contrast, was thinly built and had honey blonde hair that was dulled with age. His flat cap pulled down which was frayed from years of use

I observed as they unloaded trinkets and treasures from all over the continent.

Wonders that gleamed brightly in the glowing sunlight. They weren't from here that's for sure, people familiar with this terrain would take more care keeping their valuables hidden from the thief. They, however, seemed unaware.

"hey!" atlas hollered.

I pivoted my head round wondering why he'd so furiously addressed them.

He was fiercely stomping over to the couple.

It would look suspicious if I told him they weren't the thief so I followed along guiltily.

"how did you acquire all these cultural artifacts?"

"we travel the world and collect various items to sell elsewhere" the woman said with a toothy grin.

"and where may I ask is your permit or are all of these priceless artifacts stolen?"

The man looked appalled.

"how dare you accuse us of such a sin, we have never stolen an item in our life times we are honest and hardworking individuals and I find it very rude that you would come to that conclusion just because we look poor."

Atlas seemed very on edge.

The man slammed a certificate of international travel onto table, resulting in some items falling over which the woman quickly resolved.

Atlas' face swam in the seas of regret as he seemed dreadfully ashamed of his actions. He apologized for his accusations and dragged me away a bit too quickly for my liking.

We sat further away from usual due to the shame atlas felt.

"why did the guards want you?" He began the conversation with.

"I honestly don't know they must've thought I was someone else." I answered

He was reluctant to drop the subject

"their gullible but even they know who their after"

I swallowed before answering.

"everyone makes mistakes, they probably lost a bet and was to prideful to not go through with it."

He nodded, carefully studying me before ignoring the subject. In this time of silence, I began wondering about his finger, it was definitely a blood oath. I fear something bad must have happened for him to result to that solution.

The sunset arrived when I left.

Golden hues danced in the sky blending in with the remnants of the afternoon. Tonight is the night. I'm going to find out my past. I'm finally getting the goblet.

Instead of taking my usual route home I made my way to a nearby farm on the edge of the fluorescent hollow village. Here ill need a horse.

Squatting down I searched the perimeter. No fae. Just loot. I danced on the tips of my feet silently, not making a sound until I arrived at the stables.

 The horses bucked and neighed at the intruder and made it hard for me to establish a bond. That was until I came across a grey speckled Dutch draft horse. She was quiet and seemed unbothered by my presence. Perfect.

I broke her out and saddled her up. We had a long journey ahead of us.

The palace took residence in Atlantis further north from fluorescent hollow. I shivered at the mention of Atlantis, its people were known as manipulative and cunning. They take children right from their parent's grasps, they always find a way to win, if you thought you won you're wrong. Check your wallet.

I have to go through dangerous atlantion streets and find a way into the palace before I can even begin to think of holding that goblet. God this was going to be long. I'm going to need a lot of luck and courage for this.

"come on girl" I whispered still half aware of the farmers sleeping behind us.

The city of Atlantis has a pungent smell of death.

Menacing streets loomed ahead, illuminated only by a few flickering street lamps. Surprisingly the streets were quite clean unlike the people who inhabited them. My steads hooves clopped and clipped on the textured cobblestone beneath us, my eyes searched for any sign of life but none revealed itself.

I tensed on my horse. Knees strained and senses alert. Eyes. I felt eyes. Intently observing me. Probably sensing the shift in my posture the eyes went searching elsewhere bored of me already.

Not wanting to stay there I fled down the road to the palace. Up ahead vast mint green turrets kissed the clouds up in the sky.

Lavish greenery grew abundantly with flowers of all different colors, beckoning me to touch them. Ignoring the beautiful flowers, I searched for an entrance other than the wide oak doors that seemed ten men long and would definitely show my entrance.

A horse and cart exiting the palace caught my attention, there that's an entrance. Kicking my horse, I set off down the pastel stone path and into the side of the palace.

I've been informed of the plan so I knew where to go. Pulling my mask up, I headed for the royal jewel room. This was easier than I thought, there were no guards stationed or awaiting my arrival. Just an unlocked door. Maybe it made me gullible but I couldn't help but let myself in.

The goblet was positioned in the Centre of the room, the most valuable item here. Jewels and sapphires sparkled and glimmered but none compared and it was mine for the taking.

Reaching out I grasped the goblet and was nearly blinded by the amount of shining jewels. All was great in the world. I could finally see my past. Finally.

Suddenly a loud noise blared through the castle, vibrating me. An alarm. Shit. I sprinted down the hall way as fast as physics would let me. The guards who should have been at the door earlier were now chasing me. A trap.

angry cries bounced off the walls and followed me through the palace.

Their armor clad bodies struggling to keep up with my agility, as I swerved in and out of the dark crevasses willing my body to comply with me. God this would be so much easier if I could just keep his defined muscles and godly complexion away from my mind, if I was in a less stressful situation I could let my imagination come up with all sorts of things or certain body parts to be specific.

But I don't need him or his kindness anymore. I'd done it. And they knew they knew I'd stolen it. There wasn't much need for stealth I took it right from underneath their snobby noses. Id stolen what was presumably the most precious and desirable object in the whole of rose wood I'd stolen the goblet its mine all mine.

Heart pounding, sweat pumping I turned the corner expecting to await my most trusted stead, but as I came to a haggard stop I realized I was never escaping for he was there. A sly smile playing on his face as he held his blade to my throat. Atlas?

Why was he at the palace?

"ah ha, thief you've finally met your match and sealed your fate, now unmask yourself and show your highness your identity."

Slowly I removed my mask. An audible gasp spread among the men. Oh yes they all believed I was a man.

"surprise, I'm a woman"

Atlas looked as if he was struggling to take in oxygen.

"no. no you can't die"

"die?" maybe the shock gave him schizophrenia?

"quick leave get out of here before" he paused frantically whispering when a plump, aged man dressed in a purple suit that looked like it was three sizes too small and he refused to admit he was fat, arrived.

"ahh, my boy you've done it you've successfully doomed the thief. I'm ashamed to have doubted you" the presumably king admitted.

The words death and kill finally took place in my mind and my heart sunk wait they're going to kill me! Here? now?

The chains jingle like the soft bells on farther christmas' sleigh, my feet drag solemnly upon the dark wood beneath me. Termites stopped their chewing on the planks just too watch my head roll across the guilitine. I always knew I was going to die, I never knew it would be by the hands of someone I loved.

The executioner seemed to not be the only one who felt no pity for me.he grabbed the back of my neck and slammed me onto the wooden hole designed perfectly as the last pillow you will ever rest your head upon.

I hummed silently to my self as the executioner counted down.

"4"

"2"

"1"

The guillotine fell silent. So did the crowd. But the blade never came down the swoosh of metal never pricked my ears. Opening my eyes I saw atlas had the blade in his hand.

"the thief shall not die today"

My eyes widened in surprise and refusal as he pushed me out of the wooden frame and onto the cold dirt.

"I will. I made a blood oath with my father. I must sacrifice my life in exchange for hers" he gave me a loving look. I could swear tears were burning his eyes but I knew he wouldn't admit it.

He was tied to the guillatine and I was held back as the blade came down. I cried. Threw up. Thrashed in my chains. Acted like the animal they treated me as. Theyd killed him, my one truest love.

I drag my limp body to where his was slouched and flinched at the coldness of his once warm skin. My shaking hands could barely hold him up as I whispered,

"my love for you will live on far longer than death shall make it."

Chapter 16.

Atlas.

I struggled to grasp my last whips of power still clinging on to the tiny string that was all that was left of my life.

Astrid's words wrung in my head and I knew I hadn't died for nothing.

In my life I did a lot of things I regret but dying for her isn't one of them. Not confessing my love for her is my biggest.

If I could console her I would whisper lovingly, every tale ends once my love, ours too, I hope you will have a long and healthy life even if I am not in body, I will always be with you in spirit.

That was my final thought. My final thought was of her.

Chapter 17

Astrid.

His eyes were glass; the windows to his soul left grimy and opaque. Even in death I couldn't read him. His book was closed, locked and disposed of. And my pages were written in blood, cold crimson blood.

Till we meet again.

The end.

I would like to thank my family for inspiring me to put myself out there and be who I wanted to be.

Mum, dad, remi, nan, grandad I thank all of yous and more. <3

www.ingramcontent.com/pod-product-compliance
Lightning Source LLC
Chambersburg PA
CBHW020943160726

47993CB00007B/2920